PASSION

Sukhdev Kaur Dhade

SKD Canada Press Inc.
Brampton, Ontario
Canada

Published by:
SKD Canada Press Inc.
Brampton, Ontario, Canada

www.SukhdevDhade.com
sukhdev681@rogers.com

Printed and bound in Canada
ISBN: 978-1-989627-02-0 (Paperback)
ISBN: 978-1-989627-03-7 (e-book)

Passion
Passion

Love, loss, pain of separation to tolerance, abusive living
For the successive hope in the patience of culture boundaries
Across far away alone building bridges of east west nears.

No tears or bruises left evaluation in circle of relations.
Narrow windows, broken doors were the witness of those cries.

Prescription of pains held in capsule till
Last breath, justifying the past treatment.

Clouds roar thundering black storm wind
Turbulent funnels the shouting to lightening
Swallow wounds of flowing pain in rainwater of
Freedom.
Melted wounds of ignited fire
by yours owns rivers in ocean as food for
whales and crocodiles

(Breeze extracts- from her novel by Sukhdev Kaur Dhade)

Passion

Gift of power
Personal Celebrity
Present living
Eyes pry
Sweet in poetry
Song of heart

Parent
True greatest degree
Love treasure

Signed by
Passion
Untitled chapters

Love
And
Growing

LOVE
AND
GROWING

P R O L O G U E

Highest degree
Human creation
In this world
Beautiful cry of newborn
Invisible tone of magic secret
"Mom, Here I am"

A mother soul, love
Heart fills itself of
Joy with the
Hear of baby's first sound.
Mother instinct declares
In her heart
"My creation"
"My baby"
Gladly announces

Her universal
Highest degree in this world
Title
"Mother"
"PASSION"
Untitled chapters

Mother's silent eyes contact smile
Honors the highest degree
Title
"Father"
"PASSION"
Untitled chapters

ONE

Passion appears in the free
A globe dances around the tree
Sparks jump leaf to leaves
Search collect spots like bees
Slowly move in tree roots
Laugh, cry, happy, smile
Angry, jump, fall and dive
Run, fly, walk and crawl
Magic secret in a roar
"Passion Parent"

Passion power fly to sky
It may dive in ocean
Passion is strength
It may become weakness
Nature seed
Seed instincts, feeling
Love, hate, anger
Peace, and violence.

Newborn baby experience passion
As he enters in this world
Loud cry
Nature announce the arrival
To this world through
Baby's own voice
Very unique passion id
Get that moment.

TWO

Passion is a story
And a novel
In the middle of glory
Passion is poetry
And a poem
In the voice of song
Passion is a light
And a sight
In dark pitch night
Passion is personal

T H R E E

———————

Passion is power of purity
Lives in deep desire
Away from seeing
No prying
No touch

F O U R

Nature carries bucket of security
Five distributors
Sun, moon
Star, air and water

Free air to breath
Free moon to enjoy
Free stars to dream
Free sun to shine
Five water to live
Free sense

At the age of four
A boy begins school

Sukhdev Kaur Dhade

Teacher teaches numbers
A Boy stands up
Raise his hand
On one hand

Holding his first finger
Says One

Holding his second finger
Says Two

Holding his third finger
Says Three

Holding his fourth finger
Says Four

Holding his fifth finger
Says Five

He raises his second hand
Hold his fingers one by one
Count
Six, seven eight nine ten

He sits down
Take his shoes off
Take his socks off

Hold his one foot
Hold his toes one by one
Counts

Eleven, twelve, thirteen
Fourteen, fifteen

Holds his second foot
Counts
Sixteen, seventeen
Eighteen, nineteen, twenty

"Twenty-one"

He stands up, look around
Says loudly,
"No more"

Teacher, students laughed

School bell rings
He walks home
"Hi mom"
"I am home."

"How is your day?"
mom answers from her kitchen.

"Mom, teacher asked me to count."
"That's good"
Mom replies without looking at him.

Boy walks to his mother
Hold her first finger of
One hand, says
"Twenty-one"

"What?"
"As you taught me yesterday,
Counted
One to Twenty on
My fingers and toes
And here is
Twenty-one"

"What you said?"
Mother turns around

FIVE

———————

Nature system provide the security
Whether can be seen or feel.
Security is given.
Beginning of steps
First step strengths

A boy at the age ten months
He starts to learn stand up
Walks few steps
Holding wall
Holding hand
No wall, no hand
Sits right back on floor
Starts to crawl

Mother knitting
Boy tries to reach mother's hand
Instead grippes on wool thread
And walked his first step

Secret seed
Secret sense
Secret security
Blend in passion
Turns to
Secret magic

SIX

A two-story house
First floor kitchen,
L shaped living room
Family room and two-piece
Washroom, second floor three
Bedrooms and main washroom
Saturday was a Picnic day

A mother bath her three years son
Sprinkle powder and dress him
Blue t-shirt, red shorts
And white socks.

Let's go now, come down stair.

"Just a minute", he replies.

After few minutes, she calls him again.

"Let's go now, come down stair".

"Just a minute", he replies.

After few minutes, she calls him again.

"Let's go now, come down stair".

"Just a minute", she replies.

After that she goes up stair.

As soon as he saw her, he said

"Little bit left, its finished"

His black hair
Blue t-shirt, red shorts
And blue socks
Were all white
And he was sitting

Sprinkling powder
On his head

Looking at her he says
"Little bit left".

Astonish mother grabs
Powder bottle from her son

S E V E N

———————

Passion inspiration
Carries a basket of unknown

Mother lives in a house backing
To a park for children
Swings, a see saw and a slide
Fence installed by the town
Between park and adjacent houses
No entrance from backyard
To the park

Her son, age three years
Exit the front door
Of front side of the house
Ride on four- wheel plastic bike
Along pave footpath
Turn the corner to the footpath
Leading to the children's park
Speeds up and falls down

Get hurt underneath the chin
With bike's handle
Mother managed to stop
The bleeding by pressing the
Ice cold water cloth against the wound
Deep cut, medical attention needed
Mother drives the crying boy
Singing

"Let's go to hospital"
"Doctor will fix your cut."

At hospital, doctor comes
"Big cut, need stitches" doctor said
Mother should go to adjacent room.

Doctor finished stitching the wound
Nurse told mother to join her son
She saw him sitting quietly
She asked, "Was that hurting"

Yes, he nodded.

"I did not hear you crying?"
she said curiously

"Doctor was fixing me?"

While leaving hospital
She went to gift store
Bought him a toy doctor kit.

Now, he is doctor
Fixing patient's pain
In best hospital

Thirty years later
Mother cleans basement
Sees a toy medical box
Her son's voice
Touches her ears

"Doctor was fixing me"

She opens
Medical toy box
A voice beats her heart
"I am fixing patients pain"

Passion is innocent
It resides in ignorance,
Rise in integrity
Shines in intelligence
Grows Inspiration
Enjoys intimacy

EIGHT

Humans are unique
Ownership identification
Physical appearance
Habits and personality
Likes and dislikes
Passion nature
Creates
A film-story

Nature acts like director
Main characters are
Sun, moon, planets, water
Air and human life
Sun, moon, planets, water and air
Having same routine
Every day of life
Enormous power but fix
Human daily routine
Passion power

NINE

Producer God authorize nature
Distribute sunlight from sun
Moonlight from moon
Place to live from planets
Production from water
Air to breath for human

Be equal character
Human PASSION adds
Human volatility
Human carries passion
In the heart

Brain ability grows
Beyond limits 
Inside a parent circle
As long passion lives
Act under nature
Complete the unique
Life story
Assigned to perform

T E N

———

God has no boundaries
Nature has
Passion has no boundaries
Human has

Passion likes to be creative
Some unknown creation
Uniquely
Parent proud
Bow nature
Provide of ability

Seeing newborn baby
Mother showers love
Full of all her passion
To her baby on first look
Of baby through her eyes
Swallows the memory of
That moment in her heart
For all her life.

tolerance
patience

ELEVEN

A mother tells her daughter
 Full of passion
Woman could be beautiful
Full of fashion
Loaded with jewelry

Richest woman
Who has her baby
In her lap
Nurturing nine months
Inside her
Her own creation

TWELEVE

Parent passion
Basket of love
Formed in truth

Once a hunter went to forest
He saw a little deer baby
Put net on the deer
Caught deer
Put it over the back of his truck

After a while he looked through
His rear view of the truck,
He saw a deer following the truck

He stopped the truck.
Pulled his gun toward the deer
Deer ran away and hide in the bushes
Hunter could not see that deer
He left and started to drive the truck.

After a while hunter looked
Through the rear mirror of his
Driving truck
He saw a deer following his truck

He got out
Pointed his gun towards deer
Deer disappeared into bushes
Hunter could not see
clearly in the bushes.
Hunter came back
Started to drive his truck

After a while hunter
Looked through the rear mirror
Of his driving truck
He saw a deer
Following his truck
He got out
Fired his gun in the air
Deer did not disappear

Instead deer came close to truck
Started to bang on the
Back door of passenger side
Hunter did not know what to do

He speeded his truck
Drove away rapidly
Deer stood there for a while
Watching hunter drove away
And disappeared
In the dust airy road
Hunter sighed deeply

Appear of dark night
In the dense jungle
On muddy road
Hunter could not
See to drive

He parked his truck
Collected wood
Lighted
Fire ignited

Hunter napped sleep
Few hours later
Sun rose in the morning
He went to the back of the truck
He saw there was baby deer food
Lying beside the truck

He looked around
He could not see anyone
Only tree branches were moving
He looked deeply in dense trees

No body, was there except
Some windy air waving
The branches of trees
Hunter came back
Started to drive
His truck towards his town

Day was shinning
Sun was shy from
The moonlight of last night
Air was quit whistling,
Some clouds in the sky
Wandering with no plan
Rain of warm, cold hales
Swallowing the dust of forest paths
Hunter reached his town

He turned his truck towards
Meat market

It was very close to mid-day
Half empty streets of market
Shadowed in hunter eyes
Meat shop door peeked open
Hunter tried to look inside
Crossing his eyes
In the darkness
Beyond the close door
His eyes paused
On buying selling
Board prices

He turned around
Same deer following his truck
Standing beside his truck
He pointed his gun at deer
Deer did not move
He fired his gun in air
Deer did not move
He looked at his rear tire
There was something lying.

Hunter leaned to see
There was deer baby food
He got jerked
Shook shoulders
A paper dropped
From his pocket

He looked at the paper
A card given to him
On his birthday
From his children
Picture of two deer
A baby deer
A mother deer

Sky was blue
Clouds poured raindrops
Sun was not shy
From last night moonlight
Hunter backed up
Start driving his truck
Away from town

He looked in rear
View mirror of his truck
Deer was following the truck.

Hunter drove his truck
Away from town
Reached in jungle
He stopped his truck
Pulled away the net
From the back of his truck

Baby deer jumped
Out of the truck

Hunter was driving
Away from the jungle
Looking back through
Rear view mirror
He saw two shadows
Behind dense trees
Cuddling
A mother
A baby

High/low confidence

THIRTEEN

Blend of passion and parent
Advises
Pure child soul
Visual
Non-visual individual
Life necessities
Homely
Outside their circle

A parent utters
In bed-time story

A saint was sitting
Beside the edge river

Water was flowing
In full speed
Saint saw a Scorpio
Being drawn helplessly
In gush of river water
Saint stepped in water
Escaped Scorpio
Scorpio stung
Saint's hand
Jumped back
In gushing water

Saint looked at river water
Scorpio being drawn into water
Saint leaned toward water
Grabbed Scorpio
Scorpio stung Saint
Jumped back
In the river

Saint got Scorpio out of
River several times
Scorpio stung
Saint several times

Passion parent paused
Listener of bed-time story
Said loudly
"Why"

Paused Passion parent
Replied loud voice

"Habits"
"Easy to make
Hard to break"

FOURTEEN

A farmer bought
Expensive, healthy cow
From the market
For his family
He was happy
Proudly walking through his fields
Towards his home

There were seven thieves
Walking near by
They saw farmer
Have expensive cow

One thief approached farmer
Said
"Where are you taking this week cow?"

"I bought from the market
Taking to my home?"
Healthy cow gives buckets of milk"
Farmer replied proudly.

First thief left

Farmer walked little bit more
Second thief appeared
Said politely
"Hi farmer, your cow
Looks tired, week
How far you have to walk?"

"I bought from the nearby market
Taking to my home?"
Cow is very healthy, giving buckets of milk"
Farmer replied and got little sad

Second thief left.

Third thief approached the farmer
And said:
"Where are you taking this week cow?"

"I bought from the market
Taking to home my"
Give lots of milk." Farmer replied.

Thief gave a funny look and left

Fourth thief appeared
In front of farmer, said

"Where are you taking this week cow?"
"I bought from the market
Taking this to home
Very healthy cow
Give lots of milk."
Farmer replied unsurely.

Thief shook his head and left

Fifth thief approached farmer and said
"Where are you taking this week cow?"

"Bought my cow from the market
Taking to home?" Farmer replied.

Sixth thief came to farmer
Said

"Hi farmer!
Why are you making week
Cow walk,
I can buy your cow for a penny"

"I bought from the market
and taking to my home
But its very healthy cow
Give lots of milk."
Farmer replied
Farmer got very sad

Thief left saying
"Cow so week
May not reach home"

Seventh thief walked to farmer
And said:
"Why are you walking deadly cow?"

"I bought it from the market
Taking this to home"
Farmer got very sad

Seven people said
"My cow is week and ugly"
What my children will think of me?"

Old farmer got very sad
Left his cow there and left

Thieves laughed while
Taking farmer's cow

Farmer heard a voice
He looked back
Seven thieves
Taking his Cow

Farmer tried to run back
Oldness slowed his steps
A voice entangled
In his pocket
A parent cried
"Passionless judgment"

FIFTEEN

Parent trust natural
Highest place creates
Glowing advises

May not fly a kite
For child
Place for happy and sorrows
Of life
A candle of safe nest
In a dark night

No place in this universe
Parents not-exist

Parents are mirror not glass
Show pride in yourself, not bypass.

Talent, top is parent
Treat, turn is parent
Multi-task, time is parent
Talk tree of passion

SIXTEEN

—————————

"How is my baby?"
A mother asks the nurse

"Half open close eyes
Open wide, soft tongue
Very good, my dear"
Half-voice nurse
Utters back

"Boy or girl"
Mother voice question nurse

"A boy"
The answer came in higher tone
"May I see my baby?"

In blue wrapped blanket
Flowery angle face
Besides her left side
Right hand upward
Arm bend stretched outward
Moved him towards herself side

Little no preface
Baby kiss on blue blanket
Tilt head upward

Silent flesh and blood
Of her own
Calm look

Close eyes, black hair
Toy look
Soft than feather

Her hand moves
Over blue blanket in pair
Search completeness of tiny herself

Nurse smiles assurance
Adds the comfort layer in her heart
Confirm fullest of herself
Passion of joy bloomed in her parts
Complete tiny human of her
Unknown world roar and cry
Welcome in the world
Free to try

SEVENTEEN

Highest degree of all school
Creation of growing my own
Flesh and blood, a new shine
Full of hope wrapped in inspiration

Heart danced title of mother
A Passion Parent
Nature's unlimited buckets
In unknown creation
A path of unknown paths

Mind thunder cross destination
Ready as ever bestow a talent
Wing spread fly as dove
Light the passion soaked in love

EIGHTEEN

Passion's trust in nature
Deep love of creation
Trust in moon
Not in monsoon
Trust in sun
Not in sunshine
Trust in God not in devil
Because of the feeling
Passion in talent
Passion in winning
Passion in treat
Passion in taste
Passion in turns
Passion in talk
Passion in Root
Passion in Parent

NINTEEN

Passion is soul baby
You ever be angry
Soul is in around
comfort a whistle of cool

You are my baby like moon
You ever be alone
My soul will be around
To company you soon

You are my baby of name
You will have baby one day
My soul will tell in ear
From stars blessings just came

Deep love of creation
Trust in moon
Not in monsoon
Trust in sun
Not in sunshine
Trust in God not in devil
You are a passion
Of my feeling

TWENTY

Nature orders dues
Passion keeps
Responsibilities 
Sun revolves
Distribute sunlight
Moon revolves
Distribute moonlight

Universal items regular
Not a wish
Responsibilities

Parent passion
Not feeling
Responsibilities

Parent passion power
Not order
Experience

TWENTY-ONE

Passion wave
Parent warn still but came
Crazy soul lost in charm
Deadly speak fascinate harm

Parent design, not guess
Passion crush not to miss
Dreamy eyes close a while
Youth fire for a smile

Immerse ravish in the heart
Heart vast sea of part
Riding waves no mischief
Desire to passion in the grief

Collide blast sly feign
Stealing heart in the fame

Beauty crazy life of
Bloom flower not to miss
Beauty is not in wealth
Soft passion in the health

Beauty is in the sun
Night dreams bear to run
Diminish ray rob to hire
Black of shine with a fire

Beauty is in the moon
Cold shine burns soon
Blue sky dazzling star
Close eyes not so far

Ocean sings musical tide
Full moon in yearning ride
Breeze wind adding dews
Morning wake create a news

Night dreams day seeds
Open morning smiling deeds
Rivers run in the flow
Scattered run with a glow

Stars night still spark
Tremble feeling of the dark
Mirror tears on the cheek
Thirsty thoughts tight to peek

Eyes closed in glazed sun
Heart tides wait in turn
Starve passion shiver of light
Dark thought cross in night

TWENTY-TWO

Birthday present was a cake
Sixty candles on black forest make

Friends, family share to talk
Crawling babies crawl to walk

Blow of candles in dark night
Everyone was perfect right

Dancing lights were on peak
All wanted a birthday speech

Tall man stood with cane
Deliver a story of a sane

He was born in a rain
Natural bathing with no pain

He was born in the fall
On the ground with no wall 

He was born in the camp
Dark pitch with no lamp

All memories of past
Buried in heart live to last

Turning lights dried his tears
Hidden in eyes for sixty years

All was done in the tradition
Free of India in the partition

Pouring rain was on his side
Boat of freedom was his ride

TWENTY–THREE

Breeze of passion
Moonlight shadow
Twinkle of stars
Scudding clouds
Timid mountains
Chirping birds
Blush of rainbow
Sparked in the
Mirrored night
To carve

Unknown fountain
With
Broken pieces
Of feather
Unveiling the
Flickering tears
Blended to
Shivering sobs
For
Blooms of desert

To get a breeze of passion
On the earth

unknowns

TWENTY-FOUR

Fake dream true dream
Dreams rise as a dream
Dream is in nature
Dream is in God

Lovely ugly dream seen
Sour sweet also dream
Dream is past dream is fast
First step of a dream

Money is need
Wealth is also keen
Fame is not a dream
God gift hard work of pain

Mix of god blessing
You can dream in a day
Night is a different way
No possession over dreams

It is image of a think
Float rains in a sink
Pity rich happy sorrow
Drawing wish in tomorrow

Ghost laughs lovely face
Melted glacier mud disgrace
Room seats in the heart
Woven fears of the art

TWENTY–FIVE

Fire the ocean
Cool the lava
Freeze the sun
Speak with eyes

See through lips
Cotton the mountain
Cotton the stone
Stone the cotton

Run the still
Still flowing rivers
Motion the silent
Walk on clouds
Dry the clouds
Stars on earth
Passion in the sky

Run can't walk
Sing but not talk
It is passion
Not a heart
Life is traffic highway
Run stop to walk
Laugh don't talk

TWENTY-SIX

On spring day
Enjoying
Money
Power
Passion
Success
Beauty
With half closed eyes,
looking straight
One day
Counts the money, half is fake
Reach for power, half is late
Feel for passion, half is make
Catch success, half is stale
Look beauty, half is age

Turn to right
Then to left
See the sky Map the stars
Cool the sun
Measure the hurdles
Mind the mind

Move eyes
In circle
And
Real the fake
Time the late
Power the make
Polish the stale
Reverse the age

Holding fake, late
Make, stale and age
Tight in the hand

Jump over the hurdles
Wide eyes circle
A bless of parent
To their children
To handle passion fate
To time a late
To power a make
To polish a stale
To reverse a age
To be strong and brave

TWENTY–SEVEN

Make crazy not sports
Unveil wounds not in courts
Parent tells me same and same
That is a passion, not a game

Spring days are a wait
Inside the soul, purely date
Seven colors of the leaves
Open doors of matching keys

Feeling needs heart to stick
Moving fast just a click
Heart insider merely jail
Silent cry must not fail

Shouting tears of everyday
Melted shame of stony freeway
Shallow passion will not last
Blended memory of a past

TWENTY-EIGHT

Mind the heart
Not the passion
Mind nature
Not the session

Passion touch not a feel
Ever parent not a deal

Nature exist, can't fly
Dove fly with a try

Parent lives the heart
Passion seen in the part
Flourishing soul in the cry
Glow dark in the sky

Parent know happy sad
Passion plunges out the mad

Ugly lament in the heart
Craggy beats spark departs

Mind the heart
Not the passion
Mind nature
Not the session

TWENTY-NINE

Blue sky
Through the window
Breeze touched passion heart
Moonlight approach the surface

Held the mirror glass with hand
Drummed the tune of a band

Shadow was in the moon
See the image of cartoon

Cry was her smile
Disappear everything
For a while

Passion was sun of night
Moon faded with her bright

Gone with a spark white
Smile ray was her sight

hiddens

THIRTY

———

Middle of night announce a nation
All wake up for a new foundation
All fight for a win
Bearing cruelty is a sin

Everything must not fail
No one ever go to jail
Carry your own belong
Must quick without a wrong

Courage pen steps on stage
Ink speaks on a page
Garden trees load of grapes
Eagle crows dance to save

Sweet taste no single snake
Circle trees steal to take
Parent passion
Soft hidden trace
In global space

Grown pain squeezed in pcn
Dark eclipse elopes begin

Sukhdev Kaur Dhade

THIRTY–ONE

Ignite the water with a wave
Freeze the passion of the crave
Winds are hardly behind
Days are nearly blind

No need to look down
Guilty forever and ugly frown
Cry on a slippery side
Mountain on a tender ride

Sit here in a while
Open pore in smile

Curly waves are to shine
Bumping swimming is to mine

THIRTY–TWO

Passion is a story 
Story of a film
Jumps in a watery way
Running thoughts of a freeway

Poetry is in the time
Poetry in the heart of mine
Poetry is tell of old
Surface of hidden told

What today gone
What a right and a wrong
Dance of thoughts in the place
Igniting spark in the space

Feeling and cry of loss
Straight lights in the cross
No rent neither hire
Room of feeling in a desire

THIRTY–THREE

Passion bird whistling wind
Scattered feather lives in kind
Air is born not choosing
Sun risen rainbow bruising

Star twinkle sky shine
Heart soul beats mine
Water smile in fire attack
Deception lure ride in back

Clouds thunder lighting slip
Falling hair from a clip
Parent is not a choose
Creation of a nature loose
Curvy road of a mind walk
Subject of a silent talk

THIRTY–FOUR

Passion rose for success
Getting rose for confess
Rose is a sweet weapon
Haunt to teach as a lesson

Prickle throne are crying
Catch rosy color is flying
Fasten rose on the sleeve
Cover the sorrow for a please

Rose is red
Rose is pale
One is happy
One is sad
Fragrance of both is same

THIRTY–FIVE

Small twinkling
Surface thinking
Sky of power
A garden of flower

Winds of wings fly
Far away in the sky
Passion around with no air
Lonely, solitude with no pair

Thirst, but no meetings
One for cloudy greetings
Fresh cut burn hurting
Passion beats fast beating

THIRTY–SIX

True passion is not a game
Dream of justice
Again and again

Holding feeling is a shame
Repeat of song
Same and same

Dark nights loud cry
Grab of soul for a try

Passion is pure
Not a sin
No malicious
But a win

Passion is true
Passion is clue
It is a hidden story
Storm of mind and a glory

True passion is not a game
Heart, soul not to blame

Lips are tight in the fame
True passion is not a game

THIRTY–SEVEN

Parent heart here and there
Passion heart written to bear
Sun rise old and new
Dark ray unseen views

My arguments surround within
Fence spicy looks falling hence
Told not ready to decease
Broken heart keeping lease

Soft walk was a skill
Passion writes with a drill
Time run time still
Soft words was a pill

Beats closed in the night
Dreams speaks of bright
Sun shadows in the white
murmuring birds sing in slight

Passion telling what was told
Dreams are daily new and old
Pains sigh in repair
In passion parent all is fair

The vacant tells are my hopes
Lovely dreams polish scope
Yesterday's memories are a live
Write of passion glance to give

Hope tomorrow broken lies
Dressed pains exist in eyes
Promise is in passion store
Block feeling in a pore

THIRTY–EIGHT

Eyes half open
A tell of a secret passion
Passion fly with a smile
Laugh of cry in a while

Polish wing
Lovely sing
Return spring
Home to come
Lovely faces
Gone places

That was a precious time
All was your 
None was mine
Journey of a single lane
Cripple walks in a pain

It was not a ill
Parent wishes and goodwill
Passion is a parent's page
Write of unknown on the stage

Passion is parent beauty
Whisper song, spring of duty

Passion home glow of light
Countless stars in blue nights

THIRTY-NINE

What is that flow
Scattered, running in the glow
Wave in dark night, still spark
Passion parent in the dark

 Mirror tears on the cheek
Thirsty thoughts tight to peek

Eyes closed with glazed sun
Heartless tides wait in turn
Lonely passion tremble quiet
Dark beam may cross light

Flow of passion in the rain
Mix of feeling simmer in pain
Parent runs in the falls
Passion clogged in the walls

Passion parent friends of side
Fly together for a ride

F O U R T Y

Twinkling stars
Behind the clouds
Rose petals
 Escort moonlight

Breeze of passion
Dedicate parent night
Yearn together
Whom do I present?
Secrets of hearts

Musical voice
Unaware of rising desires
Catching evaporated hopes
Who do I present?
Unveiled secrets of passion parent

Monument of passion
Flaming ocean
 Frozen sun
Tresses clouds
Melting mountain

Quietness of flowing river
Who do I tell?
Unspoken words of
Enchanted passion parent

Eyes speak
Passion glance
Flaming ocean
Who do I express?
Passion parent of
Rising stars

****

Love, loss, pain of separation
to tolerance abusive
Living for a successive hope
in the patience of culture
Boundaries across far away alone
Building bridges of east west nears.

No tears or bruises left evaluation
in circle of relations.
Narrow windows, broken doors
were the witness of those cries.

Prescription of pains
held in capsule till last breath,
justifying the past treatment.

Clouds roar, thundering black storm
Wind turbulent funnels the
shouts to lightening, swallow wounds of
flowing pains in the rainwater of freedom.

Melted wounds of ignited fire by yours owns
Rivers in ocean as food for whales and crocodiles.

(extracts from 'Breeze' novel by Sukhdev Kaur Dhade)

The mother of a doctor and lawyer,
Author Sukhdev Kaur Dhade born in India.

She took her first breath on the bare ground
in the hands of a mid- wife
after freedom from British Slavery.

Her father S. Pakhar Singh Dosanjh had
no favoritism among daughters and sons.

Her father's thirsty soul in
literature and science education led her
to be writer and technical career.

At the age of twenty-one, she migrated to
Canada with Bachelor of Science degree,
teaching experience from England,
blessings and one hundred pounds
from her father. She educated herself in computers
and real estate field in Canada.
Currently she is Real Estate Broker
and lives in Ontario,
and her writings passion continues ....

****

Author Sukhdev Kaur Dhade in her book
***"PASSION"** stored invisibly silent sunlight of*
inner soul direct outburst of shell to unspoken peek

Drum breath cry echo enter in beauty of upcoming
human world, Welcome pour into a stream of
passions surrounded in growing.

Journey the passion in crawl walk of dusty
sparkling wind, bridges Individual
effect in and that shines turn from
*depth height of **PASSION**.*

Author's other published Books:
Behind the Sun
Breeze
Shishe Da Hanjhu, Roop
Robin with the Red Hat
Robin with the Magic Wing

****

9 781989 627020